Ratan Tata
The True Patriot of India

Devajit Bhuyan

Ukiyoto Publishing

All global publishing rights are held by

Ukiyoto Publishing

Published in 2024

Content Copyright © Devajit Bhuyan

ISBN 9789367954935

All rights reserved.

No part of this publication may be reproduced, transmitted, or stored in a retrieval system, in any form by any means, electronic, mechanical, photocopying, recording or otherwise, without the prior permission of the publisher.

The moral rights of the author have been asserted.

This book is sold subject to the condition that it shall not by way of trade or otherwise, be lent, resold, hired out or otherwise circulated, without the publisher's prior consent, in any form of binding or cover other than that in which it is published.

www.ukiyoto.com

DEDICATION

Dedicated to late Ratan Tata and to my beloved wife late Mitali Bhuyan who was a vivid admirer of late Ratan Tata and his ethics, values and integrity.
Author

Preface

Ratan Tata, the most renowned and respected industrialist, humanist and nationalist departed for heavenly abode at the age of 86 years. This book is a small tribute to the legend to mourn his death in poetic form. One poem represents one year of life in the world. It is impossible to write about such a tall legendary figure in few pages, yet I hope people may love and join me in appreciating Ratan Tata and his contribution to India, world and humanity.

Devajit Bhuyan
10.10.2024

Contents

1. Ratan Tata, the real Bharat Ratna	1
2. Bye-bye Ratan Tata	2
3. Ratan Tata, the true patriot of India	3
4. A true human being, Ratan Tata	4
5. Nothing is permanent	5
6. Zero balance account	6
7. When I die	7
8. Age is a number only	8
9. The big bull	9
10. Decline of marriage	10
11. Obituary of marriage	11
12. The wrong question	12
13. Where is the solution?	13
14. I am alone, not lonely	14
15. Ignore the negative people	15
16. No one will gossip your virtue	16
17. Don't worry, the doomsday will come	17
18. Space-time	18
19. Why uncertainty in human life?	19
20. Explaining the truth and reality	20
21. The war will go till religious blindness is cured	21
22. Forest of Darkness	22
23. Ostrich Mentality	23
24. This Millennium	24
25. Vulture	25
26. Opium of Masses	26
27. If you trust politicians	27
28. If you are mortal, it is good	28

29. Overcoming gravity and friction	29
30. Life without friction	30
31. Double edge suffering	31
32. Dosa versus Samosa	32
33. Dragonfly	33
34. Mob Violence	34
35. Bangladesh is Burning	35
36. Hundred grams matters	36
37. Don't worry, even if you can't win the gold	37
38. You need bricks	38
39. What is Freedom	39
40. Jai Hind	40
41. One more girl was raped	41
42. Funny revelations	42
43. Four quadrant of true happiness for ordinary man	43
44. You dislike aging	44
45. Everyone will pay the price	45
46. They will not get freedom without struggle	46
47. False propaganda of a cult	47
48. Teachers have no religion	48
49. Degradation of teaching profession	49
50. Charity begins at home for teachers also	50
51. Gandhi told Isvara Allah is same	51
52. The minority group	52
53. Technology for better tomorrow	53
54. Better not to live in the black box	54
55. Where the mind is full of fears	55
56. Is Guwahati burning	56
57. The heat wave	57
58. Let us pray to stop global warming	58

59. Create new opinion	59
60. Root Cause Analysis	60
61. No one can silence truth	61
62. Share your contributions	62
63. October Brutality	63
64. Good thing happened for humanity	64
65. Thank you, God,	65
66. Is Lebanon a sovereign country?	66
67. All of a Sudden	67
68. I am the centre of universe for me	68
69. Peace through Automation	69
70. The domain of time	70
71. An author can't bring peace alone	71
72. Civilization rises and falls	72
73. Bogey calls on humanity	73
74. The soldiers of peace and Humanity	74
75. Assamese Language of India	75
76. Celebrate today, work tomorrow	76
77. W=mg is not different for different religions	77
78. He (Jesus) showed the light in darkness	78
79. Gaza and Ukraine in rubble	79
80. Halal or non halal, taste is same	80
81. Religions needs early reforms	81
82. Who is responsible for peace?	82
83. Don't chase happiness	83
84. Girlfriend	84
85. Love	85
86. I am worried, are you?	86
Author the Author	*87*

1. Ratan Tata, the real Bharat Ratna

He was a generous philanthropist with great vision
Till the last breath, he served people and the nation
Always try to improve quality of life with a solution
Motive for profits never pushed his idea to hibernation
Seeing a couple wetting under rain for a bus to ride
His innovative mind started Nano car, our pride
Hundreds of cancer hospitals showed kindness of his heart
Only because of vision, hospitals in rural areas quickly start
An industrialist who thinks beyond profits and expansion
For every human problem he always derives a friendly solution
Covid19 period was a challenge to the mankind and business world
But with human touches, his whole industrial empire he unfold
No layoffs, no retrenchment even during zero production time
The real Bharat Ratna of India, always he will shine.

2. Bye-bye Ratan Tata

The complete man without any spouse or children
But his family was bitter, the whole of his loyal employees
The customer of services and products knows his ethics
Business for him was to server nation and people
Even earning millions, he lived a life very simple
One of the true jewels of enterprising make in India
His footprints will remain not only in industry but in people's hearts
A true hero of the world with great heart and love for humanity
He is now a legend and symbol of business ethics and integrity
A gentleman is that what gentleman does is Rata Tata
With heavy heat that nation and people are saying bye-bye Ta-Ta.

3. Ratan Tata, the true patriot of India

The name is enough, no need any citations
His wealth was his trust on India's determinations
Whether you drink a cup of tea or coffee or yogurt drink
His name everywhere in India you can think
While driving a car or flying in the sky to your destination
In every walk of life Ratan Tata has contributions
The poor patients of a remote village can now get cancer treatment
Not long ago, cancer treatment for poor was life displacement
Tata was philanthropist with generosity and kind heart
People respect and work dedicatedly for projects he start
In the sphere of Indian life, he was more than an industrial tycoon
His spirit spreads throughout the country like monsoon
Everyone is showing respect to this real builder of the nation
In future during difficult days his ideals will give us inspiration.

4. A true human being, Ratan Tata

He was not merely an industrialists and businessman
With human values, honesty, ethics He was a human being
Honesty, integrity, ethics and values, pillars of Tata Empire
That is the reason why Tata is respected in both the hemisphere
Protecting investors' money may be his goal
But for development of India is always in his soul
During rough days of the Tata group, he proved as best captain
With innovation and sustainability, he infused solution
Every family member of Tata group is now crying
Even the street dogs in his memory stopped playing
A real and true followers of "dog-fox-donkey's soul is Ram"
In India and world millions of his followers will remember him
Though he departed for heavenly abode at eighty-six years
But his achievements out weight his longevity, million eyes shedding tears.

5. Nothing is permanent

Nothing in life is permanent
Everything is transitory, temporary
My beloved home, my beloved school
I left long back, only memories remained
The beloved college, I left one day crying
The best friends of school all disappeared
Father, mother, uncle everyone vanished
Few generations of our beloved dogs and cats appeared
Even after knowing everything temporary
People think I will not die, and will live forever
Their wealth and money even at eighty they don't want to share
For the society they want everything, but scared about giving
Greed and lust is never ending human attitude and character
Profiteering in every step, is humans' mission and charter
Realizing that soon I may also die can make life smarter.

6. Zero balance account

You may think life is a fixed deposit account
Or for you, life may be a savings bank account
But reality is that life is a zero-balance current account
At the end even if you save, someone will enjoy the amount
With your death, nominees will become rich and affluent
Their behaviours and lifestyle will be totally different
The interest on your hard-earned money will stop to grow
In dead man's account money cannot flow
Enjoy your zero-balance money before becoming zero
If you have enough in account, live a life like a hero
Save only as much as you need for food and health care
For you, chances of building a Taj Mahal in your name is rare
So, while living to your own life always be fair.

7. When I die

When I die, someone may cry
Someone may become shy
To shed tears, someone may try
Leaving the coffin, someone will fly;
But nothing is important for me
From worldly things, I will be free
Neither insult, nor respect, I can see
My own ego and self-esteem can't hurt
Only different journey, others will start
If I am rich without any wish or will
My wealth, someone will try to steal
To show others, they will give up meal
In the funeral prayer, they will show zeal
People will appreciate the ritual feast
Someone will comment, lamb curry is best
Few others will say, river fish has better taste
But nothing matters for me after death
To do rituals for me is only people's faith
I don't know whether my mother did birth
With my departure, will also vanish my pith.

8. Age is a number only

When you are eighty plus, age becomes a number
No one will be bothered even if you don't go further
Whether you die at eighty or ninety is immaterial
After ninety you are not going to be any more social
Going out of home will be difficult and not practical
Family will be happy if you die before becoming bedridden
Paralysis and dementia after God should forbidden
It is more comfortable to die after eighty-five all of a sudden
Everyone will praise you that you never become a burden
After eighty, age will be number without any contribution
Whether eighty or ninety or hundred, I don't find differentiation
Even if the number is higher, no value for anyone after departure
Better if your young appearance, family and friends remember.

9. The big bull

The big bull generally dies in the slaughterhouse
In the trap die the fat and healthy mouse
Whether Rakesh Jhunjhunwala or Harshad
For none the death or people bothered
Steve Jobs or Lady Diana not exception
To stop departure, money can't give solution
Even uncertainty principle cannot predict future
Anytime, anywhere, even your new tyre may rupture
Don't bother too much about your cash tomorrow
Enjoy today with the family, even if you have to borrow
Love today and express it now even though you are big bull
If you keep even these things for tomorrow, you are a great fool.

10. Decline of marriage

This is cyber age
People dislike marriage
Living together is better
Only companionship matter
The child is a liability
Going down male fertility
Lesbian couple is no more taboo
Gay population is growing like wild bamboo
This world is maintaining population growth
For developed countries, work force is worth
More and more people are happy with pet
Outside home people prefer only to date
AI is now giving better robots as companion
To save old social order, there is no solution
One day civilization will collapse on its own weight
Till then, to save marriage, some orthodox will fight.

11. Obituary of marriage

During old age marriage was not for companionship
Marriage was to multiply human in a structured way
Slowly marriage became the centre of the family life
The core of the family was opposite sexes husband and wife
And thus, continued civilization and also strived
Remaining out of wedlock was considered unholy
Unmarried would be pushed to the hell accordingly
Only saints and sages remained unmarried
They were considered to be wise and society's friend
The sexual life of monks and sages kept under the carpet
The married female's duty is to fill up the children basket
Male's job is to take care that no womb is empty
Girls were forced to marry immediately after puberty
With education and economic empowerment females are now bold
It is difficult to push them to slavery under the marriage and hold
The future of marriage is now uncertain with passing of every century
Yet no social scientist can write today marriage's obituary.

12. The wrong question

Who will bell the cat
Was a wrong question
Old rats are used to status quo
They lack innovation and new ideas
Most of the time part of the problem
Not trying to open the black box
The right question would have been
How to bell the cat, where and when to bell
Many possibilities the young rats would have told
Some of the possibilities the team could have mould
In the team, never ask who will do
Path to the solution it will make slow
Rather ask how to do it to the team
It will change the whole game
Someone would have been certainly belled the cat.

13. Where is the solution?

A country with loopholes, potholes

Without morality, ethics and honesty

Everyone wants short cuts for success

Corruption is everywhere in full boxes

Dishonesty and bribes part of core values

Hypocrisy makes blind spots in every activity

Majority of people are without any integrity

Yet we claim to become world leader

Reforming our society's value system is better

Without values, honesty and integrity, we cannot move further

The moral, ethical and social value system needed to be a civilized nation

Only giving free meals to poor is not true civilization

Reforms needed in every fabric of socio-political life

Only technology cannot provide solutions to digital divide

No leader ever tried any moral-ethical revolution

In the caste rooted orthodox Indian culture where is the solution?

14. I am alone, not lonely

I am alone, but I am not lonely
So, I am moving forward calmly
My grips on the path, I hold firmly
I am giving my every step boldly;
People are in front of me, behind me
They are on my left and right
Yet, I am moving looking to bright sun light
Not willing to start with any one any fight
That is why my journey is very light;
I smile to the people who look at me
But allow people to move past who don't want to see
When tired, I sit down under a beautiful tree
I feel with the singing birds that I am born free;
Moving alone without being lonely is excellent
The journey has its own course and excitement
Some unknown friend offers a cup of coffee
The memory of the togetherness remains as a sweet toffee.

15. Ignore the negative people

Greed, anger, attachment, and sex are human nature
Without these attributes no one can move to future
In every walk of life, jealousy, hatred will torture
Sometimes your movements all these will puncture
Succumbing to all those will be defeated surrender;
Move on with love, smile, brotherhood and generosity
Under any pressure given up your core value and integrity
Now a days, to move forward is difficult with honesty
If required, walk with truth as a solider solitary
Look at the sun, clouds can't block it permanently.

16. No one will gossip your virtue

No one will gossip about your virtue
No one will say, you are fair and true
One mistake will override ten good jobs
Everyone will try to pull you like mobs
Your modesty some people will rob
Most of the people are honesty blind
Good virtue in other people never find
To anyone during distress, they are never kind
This does not mean that we should stop working
We have to move ahead everything ignoring
Otherwise, we will become a dead man with life
Forgive those noise makers, if you want to strive.

17. Don't worry, the doomsday will come

The universe is going from orderly state to disorderly state
So, in the infinite time collapse and destruction is it's fate
Entropy is increasing irreversibly and also the blind religion
People can discuss and debate, but there is no solution
Bigger disaster and destructions will come without any dilution
Unless we know the reasons for the existence of universe
There will always be lots of hypothesis with opinions diverse
In a hopeless universe doomed to collapse why to worry
Even if you journey is wrong to others, no need to tell sorry
Eat live and contribute to increase irreversible entropy
In the world no human is another human's photocopy.

18.Space-time

Simultaneously we are in past, present and future

This is the timeline and time's character and nature

There is nothing called unidirectional arrow of time

In the domain of time past, present, future no one is prime

You can be jailed at any time for your so-called past crime

Time no beginning so the question of end does not arise

Though after billions of years sun may not rise

The transitory stars and planet will come and go in cycles

But with them time never stops or collapse

Space-time is two sides of the infinite infinity

Matter, energy, universe all are smaller nitty-gritty

Gravity, electromagnetism, strong and weak nuclear force are products

The actual game the space-time domain can only conduct.

19. Why uncertainty in human life?

The manifestation of the universe is random in nature
Similar is the nature of human nature and our culture
Things happen randomly since beginning of universe
That is why everything in the cosmos is very diverse
Infinite possibilities of randomness about next event
That is why uncertainty in the universe is pertinent
The duality of wave and particle nature is core of randomness
Due to uncertainty, the expanding universe is under stress
The intrinsic nature of manifestation made living world volatile
That is why human life is also too uncertain and fragile.

20. Explaining the truth and reality

Galileo, Newton and Einstein invented nothing new
They had only observed the nature minutely
So, they could realise the truth and reality perfectly
The earth revolves around since begging of solar system
For millions of years no one observed movement of earth sincerely
Even sages of all times till Galileo no one concentrate on sun
The sun worshippers are also thinking the sun is always on run
Galileo observed the phenomenon of sun rise with dedication
So, he could find the truth and reality of nature with perfection
The gravity was also there in the earth since the big bang
Fruits like apples, mangoes used to fall, and men were eating
People never worried why this natural phenomenon is happening
Newton concentrated on the simple phenomenon of apple falling
He realised the truth after millions of years and astonishing
Relativity was there since creation of the universe, not a new thing
Even explained in different ways in Hindu religious text
But Einstein concentrated on movement of celestial bodies
Relativity came in mathematical format as the theory best
When we research and look at the nature holistically with dedication
Finding a simple truth can give to mankind big problems solution.

21. The war will go till religious blindness is cured

No one is willing to discuss about root cause of Gujarat violence
No one is willing to discuss about the cause of starting the Gaza war
We heard about colour blindness, but never heard religious blindness
Unless the world leaders removed their coloured glasses
No permanent solution will come to conflict of Israel and Palestine
People worldwide must accept; Jews are human with right to live
The blunder of Hitler and holocaust should not be allowed again
If the religious blinds don't treat their eyes and change attitude
The war for existence by the Jews will go on unabated
Because, they don't have a place to stand like the religious blinds.

22. Forest of Darkness

Child marriage of girls was prevalent those days
She was only six when she got married to an old man
She was frightened when a big rod of flesh entered her private part
She cried in pain but who will save or rescue her
The whole society was in darkness and women were commodities
They were sold in the market for a price along with other goods
Her cry died in the sand dunes of desert without any echoes
Thousands of years passed since that horrifying day
But still the system of child marriage is continuing
An everything in the name of religion even in 21st century
Are we civilized or blind in the name of blind god
No one knows when men will be rational wit common sense
We are still in the forest of darkness that is too dense.

23. Ostrich Mentality

Street dogs and crows are better than people with ostrich mentality

At least they are cleaning the nature as a scavenger in the ecosystem

The people with ostrich mentality only blame others but never look inside

They are the worst citizens and selfish in nature and culture

When majority of people are now becoming ostrich, what is our future?

For self, they need always the lions share without continuing

To their backbone, they are dishonest and cunning

But unfortunately, their numbers are growing and growing

If you are really worried for mankind, society and ecosystem

Do a small thing like the street dogs, crows or vultures

Don't close your eyes like ostrich and feel everything is fine.

24. This Millennium

Honesty is the worst policy
Truth seldom triumphs but defeated
Complexity is the greatness
Corruption is the order of the day
Integrity is difficult to find
To no one charity begins at home
People hate sinners not sin
The basic fabric of humanity destabilised
This is the KALI millennium
Chaos and disorder will be at peak
This is also the truth of physics
Entropy has to increase and increase
Till the doomsday comes
And a new planetary system will born
A new start will rise with new civilization.

25. Vulture

The natural scavenger is fighting a battle for survival
For biodiversity and ecosystem, vultures are crucial
In their groups they are disciplined and truly social
For the Persian community, vultures' survival is critical
But to save the birds, there is no solution practical
Villagers many a times poised them without any reason
But none of the killers were ever put inside the prison
The pressure groups working for vultures have no solution
Everyone must understand the importance of ecological balance
To save vultures, together let us take the challenge.

26. Opium of Masses

Corruption is now the opium of masses
It is not limited only to particular classes
Rich, poor, black, white, brown everyone does corruption
To uproot corruption from world, there is no solution
Doing corruption is neither unethical nor against religion
To corruption now a days people have no bad opinion
The politicians, common man, leaders, all indulge in dishonesty
Masses are not bothered about collective or individual integrity
But blame each other for the social infidelity
The perfect blending of religion and corruption is order of the day
The intoxicated masses with corruption and religion are happy and gay.

27. If you trust politicians

If you trust politicians, you are living in fool's paradise
Without bribe, bureaucrats will never allow you file to rise
In this world, for survival and progress, be clever and wise
Otherwise, in your life, the sun will never rise
For anything in this world, you must pay a price;
Apple polish and flattering are not effective as money
For politicians and bureaucrats, money is best honey
Sometimes, alcohol may help you in the journey
But sexual favour can easily change your tourney
If you still believe politicians and bureaucrats, it is irony.

28. If you are mortal, it is good

If you think you are immoral, you are right
You are in the 99 percent group of human beings
If you think you are mortal, you are right
You are in the one percent group of homo-sapiens
You know your time is limited and never wait for tomorrow
You utilise every moment realising time is invaluable
Time is the only free raw material in world with instant expiry
Mortal beings realise this and don't live life of future, that's imaginary
Only one percent group flourish in this world when they are alive
In their departure, the 99% group mourn and cries
And the 99% group try to make one percent to immorality.

29. Overcoming gravity and friction

The necessity of human life is not food but energy
In the process of acquiring energy, food is only for synergy
Actions of human life is only to overcome natural forces
For homo-sapiens other than food, no other alternative sources
So, we are bound by the restrictions imposed by natural courses
All the energy of human is used to overcome gravity and friction
At the time of childbirth nature gives everyone its indication
Walking, playing, brushing all activities must counter natural forces
In doing so, in human body, energy is the only power sources
Life is nothing but momentum of activities in coordinated ways
To counter natural forces, some of the energy comes from sun rays
Money, health finally converses in requirements to counter nature
In the domain of time, the mechanism one day collapses in future.

30. Life without friction

Life without friction is impossible
Movement will not be permissible
Ejaculation of sperms will not be possible
Even for sexual activity, friction is desirable
Without friction, the laws of physics will be in trouble;
Neither fish can swim, nor birds can fly
To overcome friction every moment we try
How there will be fire in the world without friction
Zero friction in our life is not a practical solution
When there is friction in the family, don't take tension
Try only for friction reduction and dilution
Friction may be dry, fluid, skin or internal friction
To reduce friction, always do proper lubrication
Even if you do not use lubricant, show your intention
To do apple polishing during office friction, never show hesitation
Friction will substantially reduce to your satisfaction.

31. Double edge suffering

Smart city Guwahati is reeling under dust
Bike and vehicle owners are clearing rust
Otherwise jam of the wheels is a happening must
Even under dust, vehicles are running fast
The inhaled dusts are germ free we don't trust;
When rain, there is flash flood and water logging
After sunshine the dust particles are disturbing
In the smart city residents are somehow surviving
People are now afraid of rain and sunshine equally
Polluted environment now engulfed Guwahati totally.

32. Dosa versus Samosa

Dosa and Samosa most popular snacks for Indian

In the matter of mobility, Samosa is a better comedian

The skin of Dosa is rice whereas for Samosa it is wheat

Both are primarily vegetarian, none use any meat

Flesh of Samosa and Dosa are same, our beloved potato

In preparing sambar only Dosa required tomato

Dosa can be taken as breakfast, lunch and dinner

But for lunch and dinner, Samosa is not very popular

In the market Samosa is available even in a small tea stall

Availability of Dosa is more visible in restaurants and mall

If I have to vote any one of them as most popular food

I am confused which recipe is better, but which I will eat, depends on mood.

33. Dragonfly

Dragonfly is poor cousin of butterfly
In flying, dragonflies are also not shy
To compete with butterfly, always try
Like butterfly, though not very colourful
With four wings, dragonflies are wonderful
They always attract people and remain cheerful
Children like to chase dragonflies and catch them
For young children butterfly and dragonfly same
Chasing and catching them is the real game
The number of dragonflies has gone down drastically
Even in country sides, they are not visible frequently
The wings of fairy in fairy tales resembles dragonfly
For conservation of this beautiful flyer we must try sincerely.

34. Mob Violence

Mob is a group of people without any brain
Destruction is the objective of the mob main
For destruction and killing no need to train
No rationality and logic work before a mob
Even their friends and relatives, they will rob
Religion is the major igniter of mob violence
Unemployment and poverty give mob persistence
The rational and educated don't give any resistance
Though for violence and destruction, no visible substance
Law and order, and police all become inactive
Military is also forced to remain passive
Only solution to mob violence is counter them with force
The mob violence must be finally stopped at source
At the beginning very high is public emotion
Vehicles are always the first target of destruction
Looting of shops and markets used to be next introduction
Burning of public and private property is mobs' intuition
Finally, the suffering is faced by the whole nation.

35. Bangladesh is Burning

Bangladesh is burning for its own conflicts
Killing of own citizens, medieval days reflects
Bangladesh is burning because people are intolerant
In inciting violence, role of their religion is also pertinent
They kill their neighbours in the name of omnipotent
Even after having so called Bengali culture and heritage
From the cruelty of killings, clear is the message
No other beliefs or thinking will be allowed
The path of religious dictate of mullahs must be followed
The destruction of national property will be counter productive
Already poor Bangladesh will move towards more negative
Bangladesh is already under poverty and population boom
The present violence and volatility pushed Bangladesh to doom.

36. Hundred grams matters

Sometimes hundred grams matters more
It can be heavier than hundred kilograms in store
You may lose the gold medal and the limelight
You may not be allowed to enter the ring to fight
So, always try to keep your body weight right
It is very easy to gain weight without noticing
But difficult to reduce even after weeks of walking
Body weight is important for healthy lifestyle
Obesity can ruin your life, that you want to live freestyle
Eat as much as you can for healthy life is old-style.

37. Don't worry, even if you can't win the gold

In the game, you may be the top seeded player
For your success, millions may do prayer
But Olympic is a competition of many layer
You don't know where from the dark horse came
And jeopardised you your years of efforts and game
Without winning any medal, you become lame
Your performance may not be same throughout the year
Even during the month, week or between the day
Who will clinch the gold, even the astrologer can't say
Even if you are in the competition, that is the golden ray.

38. You need bricks

To build a castle, you need bricks
To make a brick, you need little soil
To gather little soil, you must spend time
The time is your ultimate free resource
Every second, hour, day and month are important
How you use your resources is pertinent
Even if you think, you can buy bricks from market
Without money, no one will fill your basket
Money never comes free of cost, you have to use time
So, how you use your time is always prime
Rome was not built in a day, nor the house you live
For construction, lot of time, your father used to give
If you can't build a castle till going to grave
It was you fault that when you had time, bricks you didn't make.

39. What is Freedom

The meaning of freedom is too difficult to understand
Security of life and property alone is not freedom in true sense
Freedom of speech and voting rights to vote is not enough
Even in independent countries, for majority, life is tough
Social unrest makes life of common man very tough
Struggle for food, clothes and shelter is never ending process
To get education and health care is not easy even in free countries
Though successfully people protect their boundaries
Equity and rule of law in most of free countries are in books
Always subversion is done by the powerful crooks
What is freedom is an individual matter of feeling
Freedom is our birth right and to get it everyone is struggling.

40. Jai Hind

An old slogan yet very fresh and pertinent
Political freedom it brought to the sub-continent
These two words still uniting the people of this country
Irrespective of their political ideology and journey
Jai Hind is the objective, we must win the tourney
But we have yet to go a long distance in every field
The dream of real victory is still unfulfilled
Eighty crore people still look for government ration
For total poverty eradication, India has no solution
The country is only increasing its human population
One hundred forty crore people can't win a gold medal
But every day can create thousands of scandal
Quality of life in cities and villages is pathetic in world standards
Thousands of people live on the streets like barbers
Pathetic is the condition of poor and marginalised farmers
The disparity among poor and rich widening day by day
Unemployment is skyrocketing and hopeless is the future we can say
Jai Hind, Bande-Matorom let us say, today is independence day.

41. One more girl was raped

She was raped and murdered brutally
Politics started on the dead body fiercely
No one is bothered why rapes are still continuing
All politicians are giving reply as a fox cunning
Some are trying to save the rapist for political reason
Others are trying to blow up the incident without solution
The civil society is in hibernation like Kumbha Karna
Only fellow doctors are protesting for the dead girl
No one knows whether the culprits will come under trial
People and media will forget the incident soon
Another girl will be raped under the light of full moon
Things like rapes will continue as usual in this country
Unless all citizens join hands to break political boundary.

42. Funny revelations

God revealed too many things only to a single person, not in a meeting

But didn't reveal that on liquid gold he was standing

Discovery of petroleum none of his followers unfold

God was busy telling how many wives male should have

From the muddy pond, every morning, humanity God save

God is so cruel that he ordered killing of all non-believers

But the non-believers only found the liquid gold treasure

God didn't reveal about North and South America

Poor knowledge God proved as he didn't mention Antarctica

In the revelations no mention about evolution of species

After a long time, about natural selection, Darwin decides

A medieval God revealed only revealed knowledge of that time

God's intentions for revelations were not scientific, yet it shine

May be God knows humans are the intelligent foolish creatures

No point in revealing to tiger or eagle, with empty stomach, they will not go for prayers

Everywhere in the world the patterns of the revelations are same

During old days only God played the revelations game

To reveal new things, now a days God is reluctant, or he became lame.

43. Four quadrant of true happiness for ordinary man

When you are healthy, wealthy and wise, you are successful

Health, wealth, wisdom and success makes life beautiful

Happiness becomes a way of life, not like sinusoidal wave

Total happiness with success makes man generous and brave

You realise the importance of charity and doing good to mankind

The purpose and meaning of life become easy to find

Health, wealth, wisdom and success are the four quadrants of true happiness

It is true, renunciation of materialistic life can also give mental pleasure

But happiness through renunciation is a completely different treasure

Only sages and people like Gautam can become truly happy through this route

Achieving total happiness by an ordinary man through this path, I have a doubt

The so-called modern-day gurus are doing fraud in the name of spirituality

Majority of those are selfish clever people with doubtful integrity.

44. You dislike aging

Whether you like it or dislike it
Whether you noticed it or not
Whether you want to die or not
Every moment you are greying
Every day you are becoming old
Your good morning is diminishing
Towards death you are running
People say age is only a number
To death one day they also surrender
Make every good morning a good night
You are aging, tomorrow will be right
One can only make today bright
With aging process do not fight
Tomorrow you may not see light.

45. Everyone will pay the price

Neither I am a rose, nor I am thorn
Neither I am a butterfly, nor I am a bee
Neither I am a tortoise, nor I am a horse
Neither I am an eagle nor a crocodile
I am a two-legged unique creature
Neither can fly, nor can swim
Can't run fast life four footed animal
But I can think, innovate and do things better
On my actions, hangs all living being's future
Yet I am careless because of my greed
I destroy trees and animals' habitat without need
One day my reckless activities will bring dooms day
No one will have any innovative solutions to say
For my mistake, prices, every living being will pay.

46. They will not get freedom without struggle

They are barred from freedom in the name of religion
They are forced to strict dress codes in the name of tradition
They never protest because their brains are washed in childhood
Their attitudes are wired as per requirements of middle age
Killed brutally by male chauvinist who ask for freedom and liberty
Even their own women flocks never show with them solidarity
Because the vision of majority was blinded long back
Giving birth to child and comfort to man is their only task in world
Reforms will always be restricted by muscle power of relics
It suits the kings, rulers, religious brokers to lead luxurious life
They are happy with their harems in deserts and few with four wife.

47. False propaganda of a cult

None of the billion's member cult condemned Laden, Hafiz
None condemned the massacres of innocent Israelis
Yet some claims that the cult is working for world peace
To wipe out all other faith, they are in a continuous race
What the prophet told can never be changed even a thin hair
As the prophet said, killing of innocent Israelis is just and fair
But they forget Newton's third law about equal and opposite reaction
The cult leaders are responsible for what is happening in Gaza
For self-defence, the Jews are now destroying tunnels
And the cult members from worldwide saying, Jews are cruel
You never condemned any violence from the cult, rather celebrated
When the counter violence hit you, for false propaganda you united.

48. Teachers have no religion

Money has no caste, creed, colour and religion
Teachers must have in schools the same position
The teaching fraternity should be above social boundary
Specially teachers of a non-religious modern country
Religion should not be the centre stage of education
Science, technology, ethics, values should get higher position
Religions can easily divide people only for blind faith
Teachers can unite all going above unscientific myth
Internet, computer, smart phone, AI are above religious barrier
For all technologies teachers are the universal carrier
Europe and America is advance country not for religious teaching
But with science and technology, people are integrating
The culture of scientific mindset, only the teachers are propagating.

49. Degradation of teaching profession

Teachers are part of the social ecosystem

So, morality and ethics, they have also abandoned

Teaching is now like any other profession

This has led to the value systems degradation

The core concepts of teaching profession in dilution

To establish the old glory of teaching there is no solution

The teacher with non-impeachable character no more exists

To save value system, few teachers efforts now don't persist

Teachers are no more role model for new generations

They put software, internet, AI in the same parlance

Selling of degrees and certificates is common in the country

Coaching institutions treat students as eggs laying poultry

Teachers can be easily bribed unlike the AI operated machine

Majority of teachers are not interested to enhance own learning

Overall degradation now pushed teaching profession backwards

Teachers must work for re-establishing teachers age old glorious rewards.

50. Charity begins at home for teachers also

Teachers are neither priests nor traders
They are also not coaching vendors
The moral standards of teachers going down
Majority of teachers are not respected in the town
They themselves sold their glorious crown
Teachers are also human beings needing money
But to earn money, they should not lose the tourney
It is their own responsibility to gather honey
If it is difficult to move, you should not take the journey
Ethics, morality, honesty is important in teaching kidney
No one can re-establish the old glory of teachers, they have to do
Along with them, millions of their students will also go
Teachers must take leadership in imparting moral and ethical value
Slowly and steadily the whole society will notice and follow
Charity must begin at home, before others swallow.

51. Gandhi told Isvara Allah is same

God is Allah, Allah is Bhagawan and Krishnan
Isvara, Allah, Ram is the same God's name
For different name, prophets we should blame
We don't know the actual name of the omnipotent
To verify his name in his birth certificate is pertinent
Even his biometrics is not available in rock fossil
Like dark energy, from begging he was invisible
The bodily God is only imagination of human mind
Unlike fossils of dinosaur no bodily God's fossil we find
He may be hiding or absconding, the result is same
The frauds when caught by police play the same game
But the priest of all religions till now failed to trace him
That is why in his name crime, violence, hatred regime.

52. The minority group

They stick to the holy book claiming all past, present and future knowledge is there

The other group rejected the concept and accepted the law of change as fair

The minority group was prosecuted as disbelievers and for their infidelity

Most of the disbelievers were thrown out of the desert and their homeland

But the truth they have believed for several hundred years they defend

The believers used the swords to change the attitudes and mindset throughout the world

Many destructions and genocide in different countries and faith were unfold

The concept of one book contains every knowledge of universe forcefully sold

The history of misery and sufferings of the small group believing change remain untold

With science and technology, the small group is now empowered to resist the orthodox

Surprisingly, the world community is aloof for fear of suicide bombing intolerant players.

53. Technology for better tomorrow

Technology failed to eradicate poverty and hunger
Manufacturing thousands of nuclear weapons is a blunder
New technologies are invented to kill innocent people
To kill an unarmed man through technology is simple
Due to overweight of technology, civilization may cripple
Yet, without technologies, we would have been in dark age
Every new invention in the world always opens new page
How we use technology is up to the choices of humans
In use of communication technology for killing, nations must restraint
Technology of fire, wheel, computer always for better tomorrow
The misuse of technologies for unethical use brings sorrow.

54. Better not to live in the black box

Better not to stuck up in the black box of standard religion
Hinduism, Christianity, Islam, Buddhism give same opinion
All developed with the same God hypothesis and conduct
Present day chaotic social world order is their product
Instead of working together for mankind and living kingdom
Religions quarrelled among themselves to expand own fiefdom
With true spirit and brotherhood for humanity they worked seldom
Let new generations think out of the black box for new paths
Integration of religion through open mindset be new maths
Inside the back boxes, faithful will stick to their religion as best
A modern new concept with technology will not get chances to test.

55. Where the mind is full of fears

In every walk of life, my mind is full of fear
In this world of religious people, no one is dear
I am afraid to walk alone, even during the day
Any moment, anywhere, I may be robbed on the way
Someone will try my cell phone, someone my gold chain
I am unsafe even if I am under an umbrella during rain
Not to speak about a sleeper class journey by train
While walking alone in the forest, I am more afraid of man
A homo sapiens may appear suddenly, I have saved myself if I can
During night I can't think of walking alone in midnight
Unless I am having a weapon to save myself and fight
Even in the city of New York, at night, might is right
The fair sex may be abused or harassed by any stranger
To travel in the night even in bikes, for them, there may be danger
Majority of people in the world live within the religious boundary
But in reality, and behaviour even the so called priests in quandary
In the third world religious countries even, foods are not safe
Adulteration and to cheat people, every shop keepers chafe
My money is not safe even in the bank, how can I carry cash
The credit card fraud done to me, in my mind still fresh
My mind is with fear in the crowd of Kumbh mela also
Better I prefer not to travel to temples, thinking freely solo.

56. Is Guwahati burning

(Recorded highest September on 23/09/2024)

Is Guwahati burning during spring September
The dew drops on grasses we still remember
After the sufferings of flash flood and dust storm
Now at forty-degree, water of Guwahati is too warm
The white jasmines are now absent in the city
For the citizens of the city nature is showing pity
Already Guwahati is a polluted city and not liveable
More human population in the city is now not feasible
Extreme heat may bring temperatures fluctuations
Too clod during winter months many create strange situations
As of now Guwahati is burning under extreme heat wave
Our beloved Guwahati of twentieth century how to save?

57. The heat wave

The nature is now showing its furry
Humans must apologise saying sorry
Temperature is increasing every year
Yet for destructions, humans don't fear
For homo sapiens concrete jungle is dear
Housing is needed for every citizen
Cutting of trees never get resistance
Ecological balance man has badly destroyed
For other livings mother nature is now annoyed
Flash floods in deserts once unbelievable
For nature pushing cars like paper boats is feasible
Human can destroy nature cutting hills, making dams for comfort
To balance the destructive forces, its own course, nature resort.

58. Let us pray to stop global warming

We used to pray God during childhood for rain
God hypothesis taught us that God's desire is main
Shouting on every household, God hypothesis train
If rain comes, credit goes to the almighty
But if no rain comes, people forget it silently
As per God hypothesis, he is responsible for global warming
He directed environment and ecology for rapid changing
Rather than blaming development, as it is also wishes of God
To stop global warming, under the sun we should pray him for his nod
He only knows his planning about homo sapiens and world
As per his wishes and planning, in the world things will unfold
The path to satisfy him, to some prophet he might have told.

59. Create new opinion

We are safe in our homes not because of age old religion
Nor we are safe because of religious values and ethics
We are also not safe because of the all-powerful almighty
We are safe because of the laws framed by Republics
Our property is protected not for fear of God or his punishment
Rather our lives and properties are protected for fear of police
Remove police and military for a few days and see the results
Everywhere there will be robbery, murder and unruly mob
Any moment even the most religious people will be robbed
The fear for God and religious values has no place nowadays
For fear of human beings, the God might be hiding somewhere
Along with God hypothesis, communism has also failed
Democracy in most of the religious countries derailed
Only solution is new hypothesis with out of box vision
For this among new generations, we must create opinion.

60. Root Cause Analysis

People dislike root cause analysis
Because it always brings out the truth
Truth is in most of cases harsh and bitter
It derails apple cart of mask wearing gentlemen
Many Brutus came out to the notice of public
There is hue and cry for searching the reality
But every time, everywhere, truth remains solitary
Every part of society wishes to bury truth for own reason
Finally, the truth is pushed behind the veil as treason
Truth revealed immediately has intrinsic value for justice
After years, it has value for discussion, no need to notice.

61. No one can silence truth

You can't silence truth by blocking in digital media
You can't burry the sun in a pool of muddy water
The world has witnessed many holocaust
This is the time that we speak just and allow truth to outburst
In twenty first century majority of people know the truth
But their conscience was misguided and on wrong foot
If the intelligent people don't come forward
For the humanity, destruction will be the reward
I will always tell a spade a spade and thief a thief
Even though among fake societies, it creates mischief
Remove your coloured glasses of medieval age
Try to write in the history of modern world a new page
When you are out of the black box and far in the horizon
You are not going to block truth speaking netizen.

62. Share your contributions

The DNA of human developed as pound wise penny foolish
That is why sometimes people are low and sometimes bullish
The war mentality is embedded in the DNA code to continue
In the ages and civilization only changes the war venue
Without war, civilization cannot progress due human mindset
The capability of warfare and technology human must test
From bow and arrows to swords progress was slow
With the invention of gun and bullet in the war field came glow
Nuclear weapons showed its might in second world war
No one knows about the third world war and it is how far
The small trailer of war will always continue here and there
Yet for peace and brotherhood, your contribution try to share.

63. October Brutality

Some people concentrated on one book for knowledge
Change of technology and evolution others acknowledge
The result is now totally different from medieval days
Thank Allah, he put the sun under mud and for them no rays
With borrowed technology, they still continue aggression
To destroy their backbone with modern technology is the solution
Under pressure from others there should not be dilution
The world needs, terrorist's total elimination
Unaffected countries will say for peace and tranquillity
But most of the countries were mum during October brutality.

64. Good thing happened for humanity

From world, Isreal removed some bad element
Yet to praise their bravery, some countries are silent
Because of brave Jews, the world can now sleep well
The excellent job of the Israeli heroes time will tell
The remaining terrorists also Isreal should kill
The Israeli army should continue their war drill
India should help them with materials and skill
The deformed DNA of orthodox people never change
So, by surgical strike and war, the mankind has to manage.

65. Thank you, God,

Thank you, God, Allah or whatever name people call,
This time in middle East nations, your reactions are small
Sixteen hundred years ago, you never tried to protect the Jews
Even during second world war, you never heard their cries and hues
Now throughout the world, their number is very small
But for survival, they have taken own way and not miss call
They are not going to repeat the age-old mistake once again
If they do so their identity, they will not be able to retain
Thank you, God, for not taking side of intolerant people
Jews have realised that offence is best defence your rule simple.

66. Is Lebanon a sovereign country?

Is Lebanon a sovereign country or puppet of militants
From the Lebanon against militants there was no resistance
Israel is forced to the war by the militants without any reason
Lebanon should take proactive action for a permanent solution
Lebanon should push back militants with an agreement with Israel
Then only possibilities of a permanent peace will be there
Only solution is total disarmament of militants in Gaza and Lebanon
Arab countries should immediately stop them any ammunition
America is doing right thing in supporting Israel wholeheartedly

Let new president of America come and resolve the problem personally.

67. All of a Sudden

Human beings once died means gone forever
No one had ever come back from heaven or hell
Neither Rama, Buddha, Jesus or Muhammad
Death means end irrespective of how powerful you are
Even spending billions no one can come back with the same body
The rebirth, souls and incarnation all are myths and beliefs
Wired to our brains by environmental factors and education
Everyone die with the hope of heaven and rebirth
Even after knowing the past record of billions of deaths
In the illusive heaven and rebirth, many waste this life
Don't live in an imaginary world of rebirth and heaven
Only truth about death is that, it comes all of a sudden.

68. I am the centre of universe for me

I am the proton, neutron and electron discovered by scientists
I am the elements carbon, oxygen, hydrogen and nitrogen
I am built by all these things available in the universe
I am the matter; I am the energy and duality in nature
But I am not merely a bundle of fundamental particles
I am having my own mind and unique consciousness
So, I am the fundamental particles, but I am different
In the infinite universe, for me, I the centre
I am the observer for me and without me no existence of universe
Yet, I governed by natural laws and uncertainty principle
My wave function or material body at any moment can collapse.

69. Peace through Automation

For world peace through automation one man is struggling
Better automation technology no one is offering
He brought rain in Arabian deserts and the dry land
Many plants and herbs in the deserts now on sand
With the army of Israel and Netanyahu all must stand
Nature had done automation for millions of years through evolution
For automation of human brains, nature will give solution
Without peace automation processes become slow
If the wars come to an end, civilization will glow
Otherwise, automation, third world war will toe
Even with best automation, destruction will not be slow.

70. The domain of time

The past, present and future manifest simultaneously in quantum world

All the three event horizon continuously with discontinuity unfold

How surprising it will be seeing our own birth, and the pain mother suffered

Funny will be to know who are in our funeral march before our death occurred

Even than people may not be able to alter the happening in time domain

Otherwise, the existence of life will be impossible to sustain

Life for humans will be life in a wonderland unknown to us

But as we will die before that, we will certainly miss the beautiful bus

Other living beings will be just puppet and slave to surve human needs

Otherwise also at present time, animals are doing similar deeds

God will be caged with the cat in the same box to know his position

For God, instead of facing humiliation, destruction of world is better solution.

71. An author can't bring peace alone

The Satanic Verses cannot bring peace to the world, author lost one eye
The pen was never mightier that the swords in Arabian deserts
The non-believers were killed randomly to create fear psychosis
And the empire expanded through the power of the swords
But finally, the empire failed to resist new thinking
Technology moved rapidly and the holocaust happened
Yet, the harbingers of truth united again to fight the rascals
A small group of people, once thrown out fought the radicals
Every time the peace efforts were thwarted
And the tiny nation has no alternative but to take th bull by horns
For the slaughter of their people also together they mourned
Now the hooligans must be taught a lesson to remember
In the world, the leader of peace will always be remembered.

72. Civilization rises and falls

Civilization rises, civilisation falls
When time comes, it gives its call
The civilisation may be big or small
Technology may be sophisticated and tall
Yet it can burst like a Russian ball;
World is now full of nuclear missiles
Under the ground lots of dead fossils
Present civilisation can vanish within a day
No one will be able to speak their say
New civilisation will emerge with new ray;
Millions of years later, new hypothesis will come
But forever this flourishing civilization gone
New species will appear with different cycles and turn
They will have own Darwin, Newton and Einstein
Civilization always come and go in a chain.

73. Bogey calls on humanity

The world initially gave a blind eye when holocaust started
Millions of innocent Jews and children were butchered
Finally, they got their homeland after a long struggle
Yet the people who drove them out even today mingle
Bombed the homeland of Jews without any provocation
Killing innocent people, the hostile Arabs think is solution
Again, and again kidnapped women and young girls
Raped them like their prophet, who showed the path
Peaceful coexistence is the only solution some Arabs don't accept
When to save life, when people resist, as if humanity contract.

74. The soldiers of peace and Humanity

O' thy brave soul, one day you will win
You are on the path of truth and commitment
But the slave traders with ignorance always try to eliminate
This time you should not backtrack and stick to your actions
The religion of intolerance and violence can't sustain
The warriors of truth will put this time history on order
No one will be able to rape innocent minor telling it God's wishes
If necessary nuclear weapons to be used to kill devils
Otherwise, they will again grow like viruses to harm mankind
All rational people around the world praying for your victory
Every democratic nation will help you to destroy devils, if necessary.

75. Assamese Language of India

Assamese is a language developed Christ was born
Even during the days of epic Mahabharata, it was spoken
The Assamese language is very sweet like Assam's beauty
The language is also very versatile with diversity
To make it visible at world level is every Assamese's duty
Naming as one of India's classical languages is not enough
To put Assamese literature in world forum is still tough
The road to Booker and Nobel prize is not easy, but rough
Translation is must for the notice of readers outside India
Nowadays it is easy to propagate literature through social media
The intelligent children must come to study in mother tongue
Then only within Assam, Assamese will spread as people's langue
Only putting a stamp by Government will serve no purpose
If the new generation with creativity, new literature does not compose.

76. Celebrate today, work tomorrow

Celebrate today for the recognition we received

But it should not end in celebration alone

Now it is duty of everyone living in Assam to uphold it

For global exposure we have to make Assamese language fit

Without follow-up work, celebration will be momentary

Celebration will remain as media and newspaper history

The momentum created by celebration should create new story

Giving speeches by politicians will die down like ripples

Every author must work hard before the momentum cripples

The one-point agenda should be creating new modern literature

Only with books in all the formats can protect Assamese language's future.

77. W=mg is not different for different religions

Gravitational forces are uniform throughout the world

The theory of relativity, throughout the globe same way unfold

Electricity is same in Israel, Gaza, Lebanon, India and Pakistan

Science has uniform laws throughout the globe without discrimination

But religions are discriminatory, and partisan based on faith

Fighting for heaven and God without any uniform rules or laws

Killing innocent are also justified by so called religious gurus

They don't have any scientific thinking for better tomorrows

War can never be holy as it involves killing of humans

Yet people became foolish, knowing, killings is sin as per own religion

So, for peace, within religious black box there will be no solution

The fake narratives of medieval age among Arabian people need dilution.

78. He (Jesus) showed the light in darkness

From the darkness of jungle rules in Arabian deserts
Path to Love, humanity and ten commandments Jesus starts
The ignorant people crucified him without understanding him
But he prayed for their mercy and protection of their kin
His teachings is still the kindly light to show path to mankind
Some people tried to move otherwise and tried for a better path to find
Clever one declared himself as last prophet to deceive people
In an ever-changing universe status quo in any matter is not simple
It is impossible to denounce Jesus and his ideas, someone to cripple
As long as we remain tolerant and love all, world will overcome all trouble.

79. Gaza and Ukraine in rubble

God is a dumb, deaf, blind and helpless creature

But without God also, humanity has no better future

God failed to stop the holocaust of Jewish since time immemorial

Now to stop killings of innocent, God became too political

As he is dumb, deaf and blind, for peace he cannot become instrumental

God never tried to protect his mosques, churches or temple

His physical handicapped condition is the reason simple

And to satisfy the physically impaired, humans create trouble

Even the strongest devotees, in the name of God never behave humble

God progressed from fire to smartphone, but Gaza and Ukraine became rubble.

80. Halal or non halal, taste is same

The lamb was butchered for meat by an animal named man

After death the lamb has no meaning how he was killed

In the name of God as halal or without offering to God

The tastes of meat remain same with halal or non halal

God has no role either to kill the lamb or save his innocent child

Man think that God will be happy, that is foolish and wild

Good that non-orthodox people don't bother the process

But some superstitious people are still ignorant and unconscious

Rationality and logic must enter religion for reforms and modernisation

If no reforms are done by intelligent among orthodox, enjoy destruction

81. Religions needs early reforms

Once they sacrificed humans to satisfy God and for his mercy
The British made laws banning human sacrifice in the name of God
But animal sacrifices are still continuing in temples and shrines
Some goddesses with animal blood also prefer to have wine
The system of widows killing on fire was also abandoned
Yet in the food habits there are some restrictions
They realised long ago with the British that changes are necessary
That is why accepted religious division of the country
The orthodox people have now no food and money to repay loan
The orthodox religious country may collapse very soon
In the evolution of civilization, only who adopt changes survive
The orthodox people should change attitude and become active
War in the name of religion has no place in this millennium
For reforms and education, religious people should form collegium.

82. Who is responsible for peace?

Such a complex ecosystem of human society
Since time immemorial, conflict and war is order of the day
How peaceful coexistence will be there, no one can say
A small spark is enough to start a dispute killing thousands
And a world war can easily kill millions without any reason
Who is responsible for peace, Russia, America or Isreal
Or the religious heads controlling so-called peaceful religions
Common man has nowhere to go, except the bunkers to save life
The United Nation is now only a paper tiger without life
Common men are mad for religion and territory of nation
In the distant future also, there is hope of peace and conflict resolution
May be the future generations will take conflict as part of life
With pollution and nature's fury, they have to survive.

83. Don't chase happiness

Don't chase the butterfly to catch it and enjoy its beauty
Sit silently for sometimes in the garden enjoying them freely
Suddenly one of them will come and will rest on your shoulder
If you try to catch and hold it, it will fly away within a moment
So, better enjoy the beauty of the butterfly being silent
Happiness is similar, you can't catch if run after for it
If you do a small activity enjoying it, happiness will click
Enjoying a movie may make you happier than buying something
Find out your hobbies and likings, you are really enjoying
Happiness is never a straight line without ups and downs
Without sad and difficult moments, happiness will not be around
There is no perfect happiness index applicable to all
Your own mindset and attitude can only give you happy call.

84. Girlfriend

How beautiful she is, you can only feel
The beauty of her blue eyes you can't explain
Her fragrance no one can appreciate except you
She is soft like the spring September dew
In the whole world she is the best among few
Yet suddenly within a day everything changes
Because relationships with others also she manages
The existence of a third person with your friend unacceptable
The triangle of trio become volatile and unstable
The most important person of life become intolerable.

85. Love

Love is sometimes butterfly, and sometimes cry
Relationship is sometimes wet and sometimes dry
In Love sunny days and rainy days come too frequently
But relationships, a small quarrel may put in quandary
People come and people go from life like day and night
Like full moon, true love in life always remains bright
When love is flying high in the sky like a beautiful kite
Hold your string firmly, skilfully and very tight
One small mistake may snatch the string
And it will fly its own becoming irresistible warrior king.

86. I am worried, are you?

Not merely climate and environment are changing

The minds and mindset of human has taken turn

Are we changing for better or worse?

Is the progress being for development or destroying nature?

Why the conflict for manmade boundaries and destruction?

Is it necessary, all the deforestation and construction?

But I am confused and can't find any practical solution

The double edge sword of population growth and development

Cutting the mother earth and nature to bleed continuously

The deserts see unprecedented rain and flood

The jungles of rain forests and habitats of animals becoming dry

The man animal conflict whose creation, everyone knows

Yet we have no ways and means, attitude to save nature

I am worried what will happen when temperatures rise in future

The rising seas and devastating rainfall will change human life and culture.

Author the Author

Devajit Bhuyan

DEVAJIT BHUYAN, an electrical engineer by profession and poet, author from the heart, is proficient in composing poetry and prose in English and his mother tongue Assamese. During last 26 years, he has authored more than 74 books published by different publishers in 45 plus languages. His total published books in all the languages counts to 207 and growing every year. Devajit Bhuyan's children's books and comics are very popular among children and adults.

To know more about him please visit *www.devajitbhuyan.com* or view his YouTube channel @*careergurudevajitbhuyan2024*.

www.ingramcontent.com/pod-product-compliance
Lightning Source LLC
LaVergne TN
LVHW041538070526
838199LV00046B/1730